Sylvie

Written by

Jean Reidy

Illustrated by

Lucy Ruth Cummins

Atheneum Books for Young Readers

New York London Toronto Sydney New Delhi

To Alexa—J. R.   *For my little Jacob—L. R. C.*

A
atheneum

ATHENEUM BOOKS FOR YOUNG READERS · An imprint of Simon & Schuster Children's Publishing Division
1230 Avenue of the Americas, New York, New York 10020 · Text © 2022 by Jean Reidy · Illustration © 2022 by Lucy Ruth Cummins
Book design by Sonia Chaghatzbanian © 2022 by Simon & Schuster, Inc. · All rights reserved, including the right of reproduction in whole or in
part in any form. · ATHENEUM BOOKS FOR YOUNG READERS is a registered trademark of Simon & Schuster, Inc. Atheneum logo is a
trademark of Simon & Schuster, Inc. · For information about special discounts for bulk purchases, please contact Simon & Schuster Special Sales
at 1-866-506-1949 or business@simonandschuster.com. · The Simon & Schuster Speakers Bureau can bring authors to your live event. For more
information or to book an event, contact the Simon & Schuster Speakers Bureau at 1-866-248-3049 or visit our website at www.simonspeakers.com.
The text for this book was set in Baskerville. · The illustrations for this book were rendered in gouache, brush marker, charcoal, and colored pencil,
and were finished digitally. · Manufactured in China · 0122 SCP · First Edition · 10 9 8 7 6 5 4 3 2 1 · Library of Congress
Cataloging-in-Publication Data · Names: Reidy, Jean, author. | Cummins, Lucy Ruth, illustrator. · Title: Sylvie / Jean Reidy ;
illustrated by Lucy Ruth Cummins. · Description: First edition. | New York : Atheneum Books for Young Readers, [2022] | Audience: Ages 4 to 8.
| Summary: "A picture book about a surreptitious spider who gathers the courage to help the neighbors she has watched over from afar—
a promising painter, a proper little lady, a mindful young man, a brave girl and her exceptionally brave tortoise"—Provided by publisher.
Identifiers: LCCN 2020037117 | ISBN 9781534463486 (hardcover) | ISBN 9781534463493 (ebook)
Subjects: CYAC: Spiders—Fiction. | Neighbors—Fiction. | Friendship—Fiction. | Apartment houses—Fiction.
Classification: LCC PZ7.R273773 Sy 2022 | DDC [E]—dc23 · LC record available at https://lccn.loc.gov/2020037117

Sylvie hung on a silvery thread from the rusty underside of a fire escape.

And though it
was dark

and damp

and disturbingly close
to the dumpster,

that hideout
was *home* to
Sylvie because,

you see,

not everyone

appreciates a spider

who calls attention

to herself.

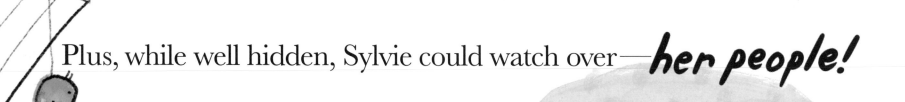

Plus, while well hidden, Sylvie could watch over—*her people!*

The promising painter with the perfect palette.

The proper little lady with the china teapot.

The mindful young man
working on a plan.

And the brave girl with the
exceptionally brave tortoise.

Day and night,

night and day,

looking with longing at that crew in plain view,

Sylvie made sure

that everything

and everyone

on every
floor were—

just so.

But lately,

that teapot sat
well below
brimming,

that plan seemed
rather bland,

that paint sat with
blue unused,

and that tortoise—
well!—
that tortoise's
exceptional bravery
seemed untested in his tank!

Was just so, just right?
Or did the four
need something . . .

more?

No! No!
Heavens no!

Sylvie put the thought
right out of her heart
because,

not everyone appreciates a spider
who calls attention to herself.

Then one day,
just before teatime,

that same sun
that seldom saw
the underside of
the fire escape—
streamed a single ray
at just the right angle.

It seemed to shine a bit
brighter

and

linger a little longer,
and it caught Sylvie's
thread in a most
determined,
distressing, and
double-crossing way.

What was
a spider
to do?!?!?!?

But then—

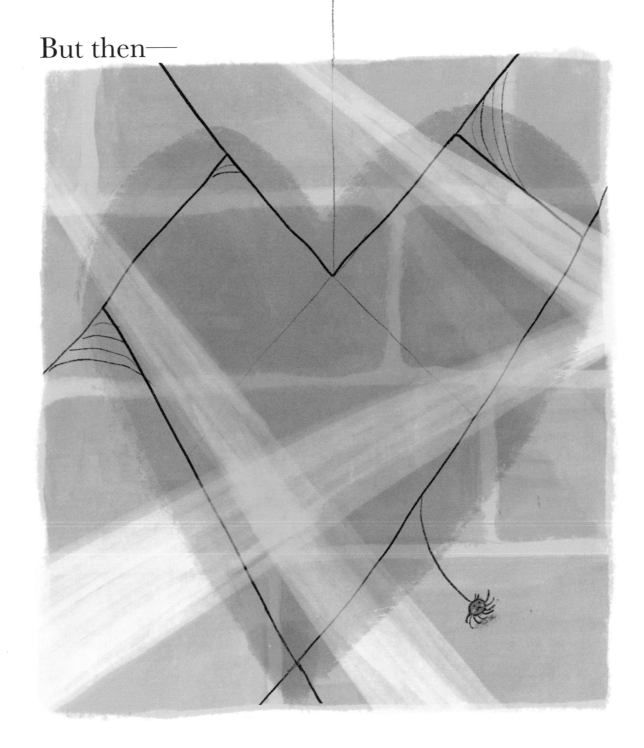

And then—

And plain as day from her
perfect perspective,
it came to her —

An **audacious, dangerous, MAGNANIMOUS** idea.
An idea that might make everything—dare she say it?—
just right!

Sylvie couldn't! She shouldn't!

She mustn't—

but . . .

So,

with hope in her heart

and the sun on her thread,

Sylvie inched into the light!

She scurried past the girl with the

exceptionally brave tortoise.

She skirted past the
young man working on a plan.

She scooted past the little lady
with the china teapot.

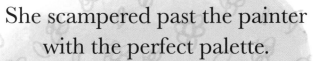

She scampered past the painter
with the perfect palette.

And then she looped and leaped and led
her people all the way up to the tip-top
of the world . . .

where soon the four
found much,
MUCH more.

But Sylvie had stopped just short of the top, watching, wondering, when—

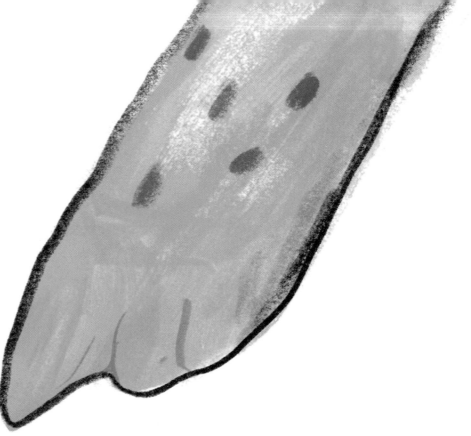

WITHOUT

!

PROPER

WARNING—

she was *warmly* welcomed.

And basking in that beautiful beam,
Sylvie was a sight to be—

seen!

That's when that oh-so-savvy spider,
with more moxie than misgiving,
sashayed straight through the
paints and

onto the plan!

And with a touch of inspiration,
some blending brushstrokes,
and a heartfelt nod, everything—
and EVERYONE—
came together . . .

just right!

Because it's true that while not
everyone appreciates a spider who
calls attention to herself . . .

grateful friends most certainly do!

SYLVIE